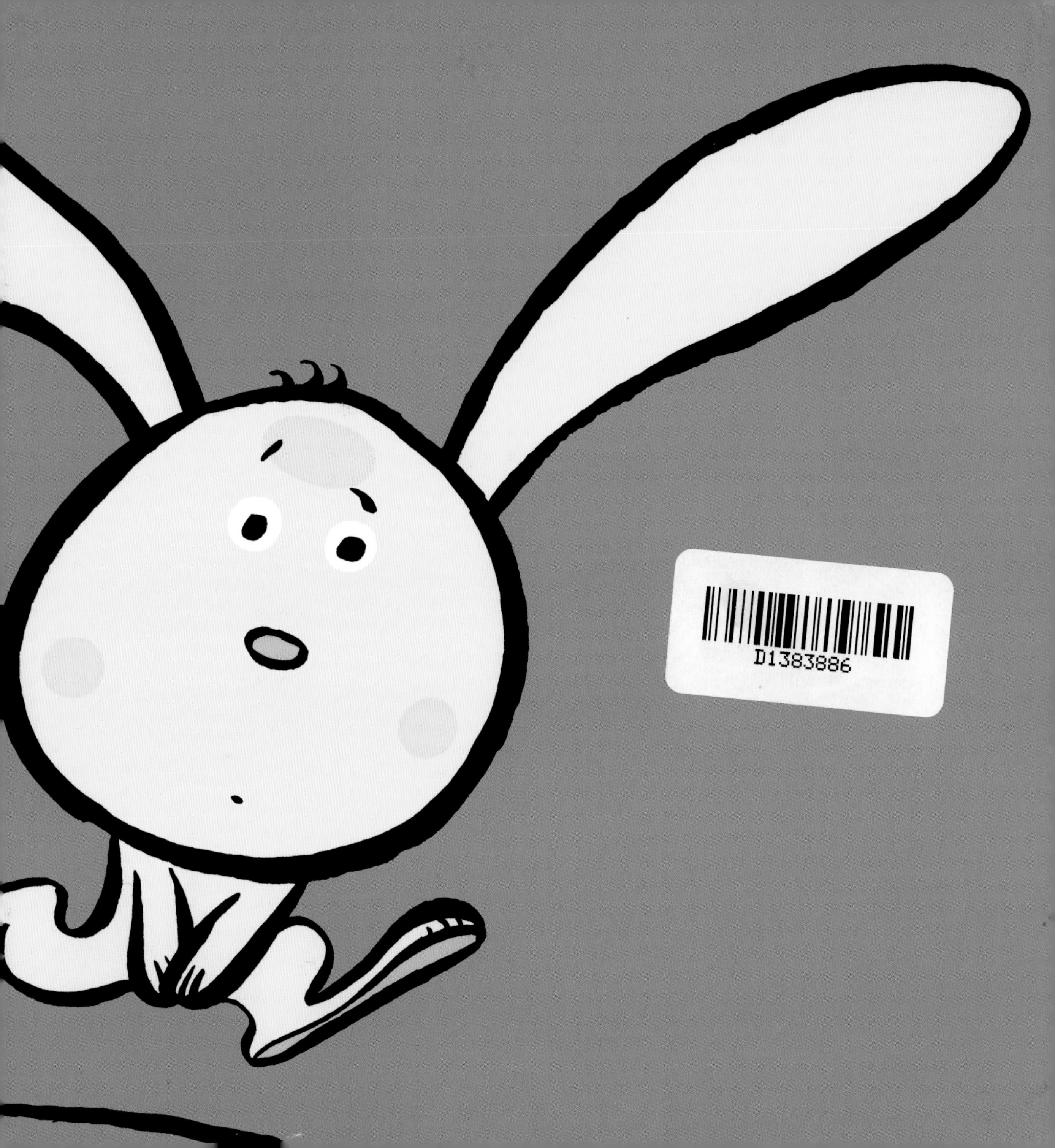

Quick!
Quick!

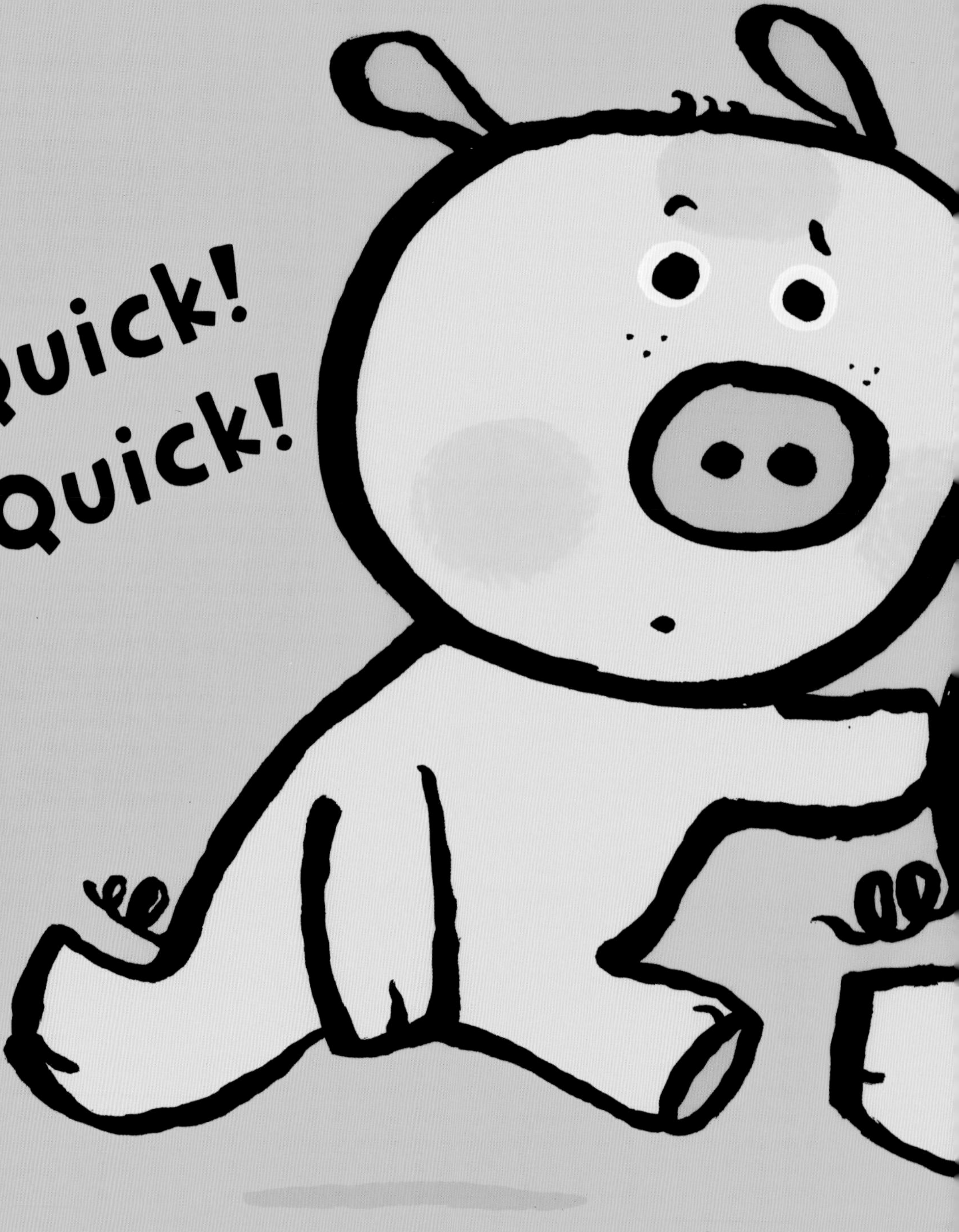

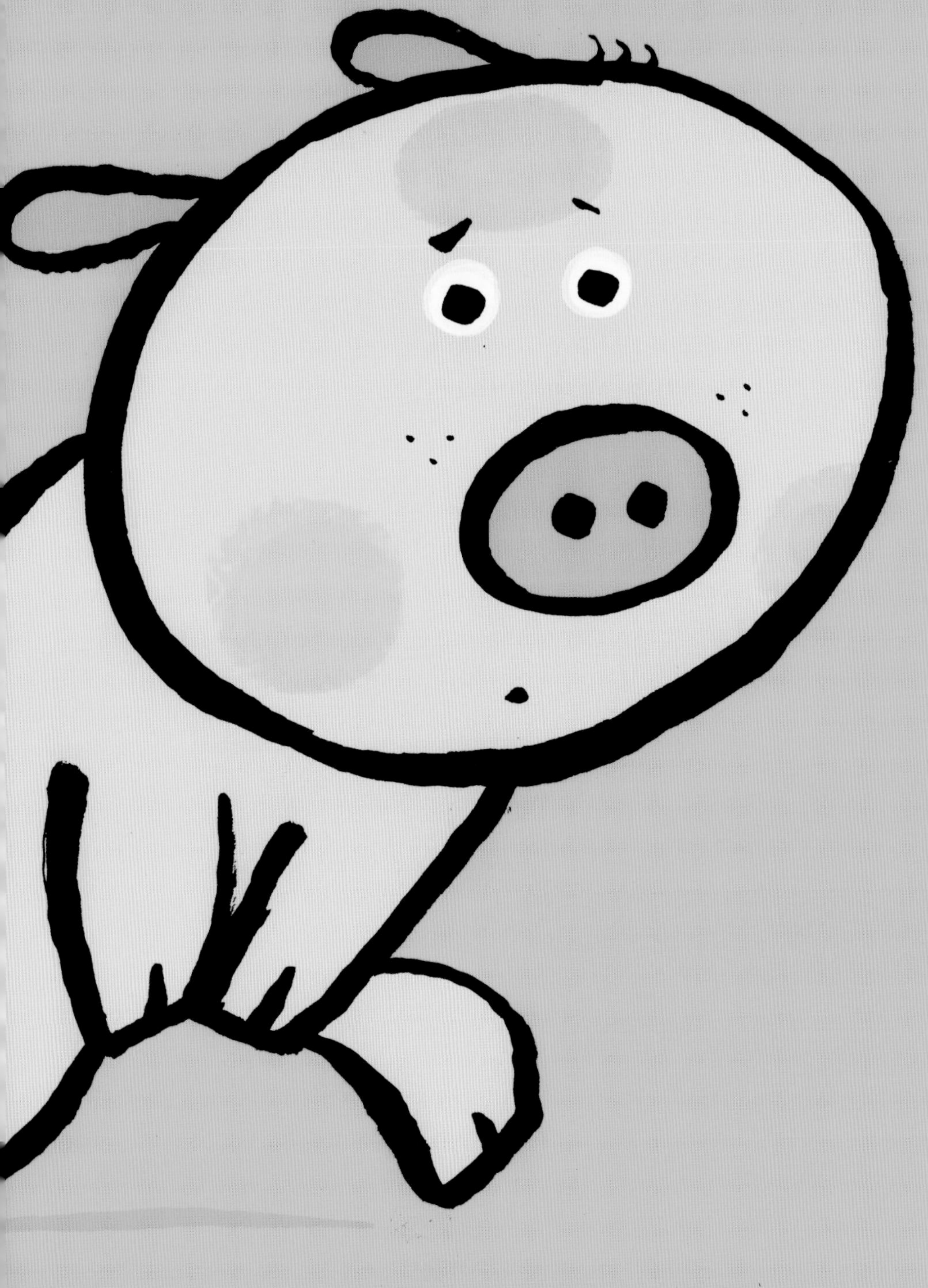

Oops!

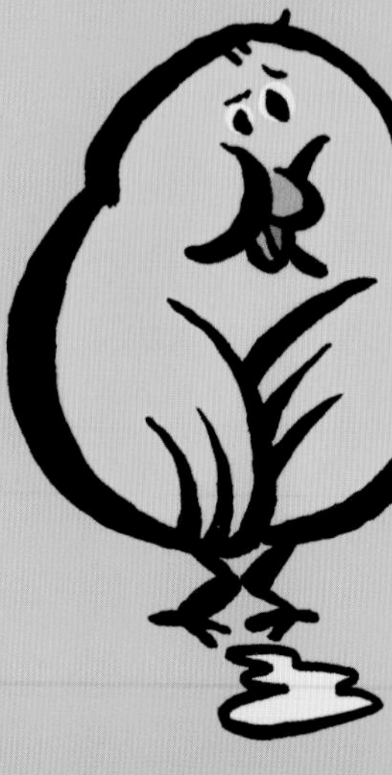

Let’s hurry!

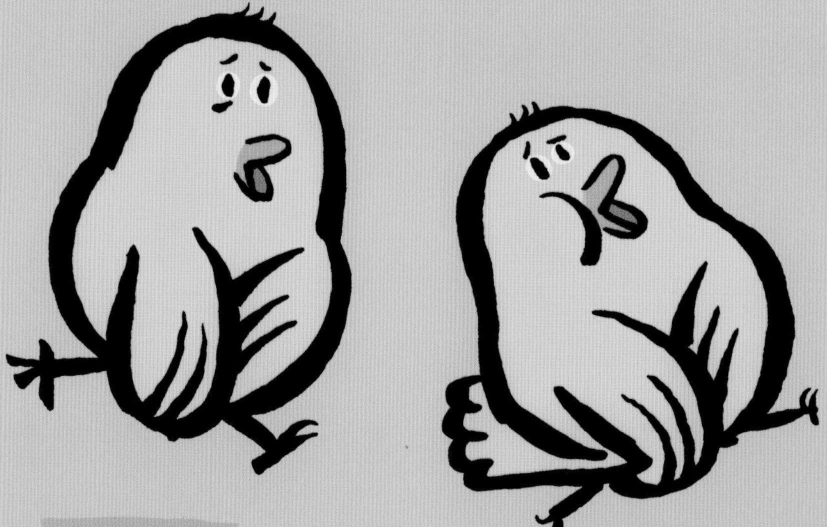

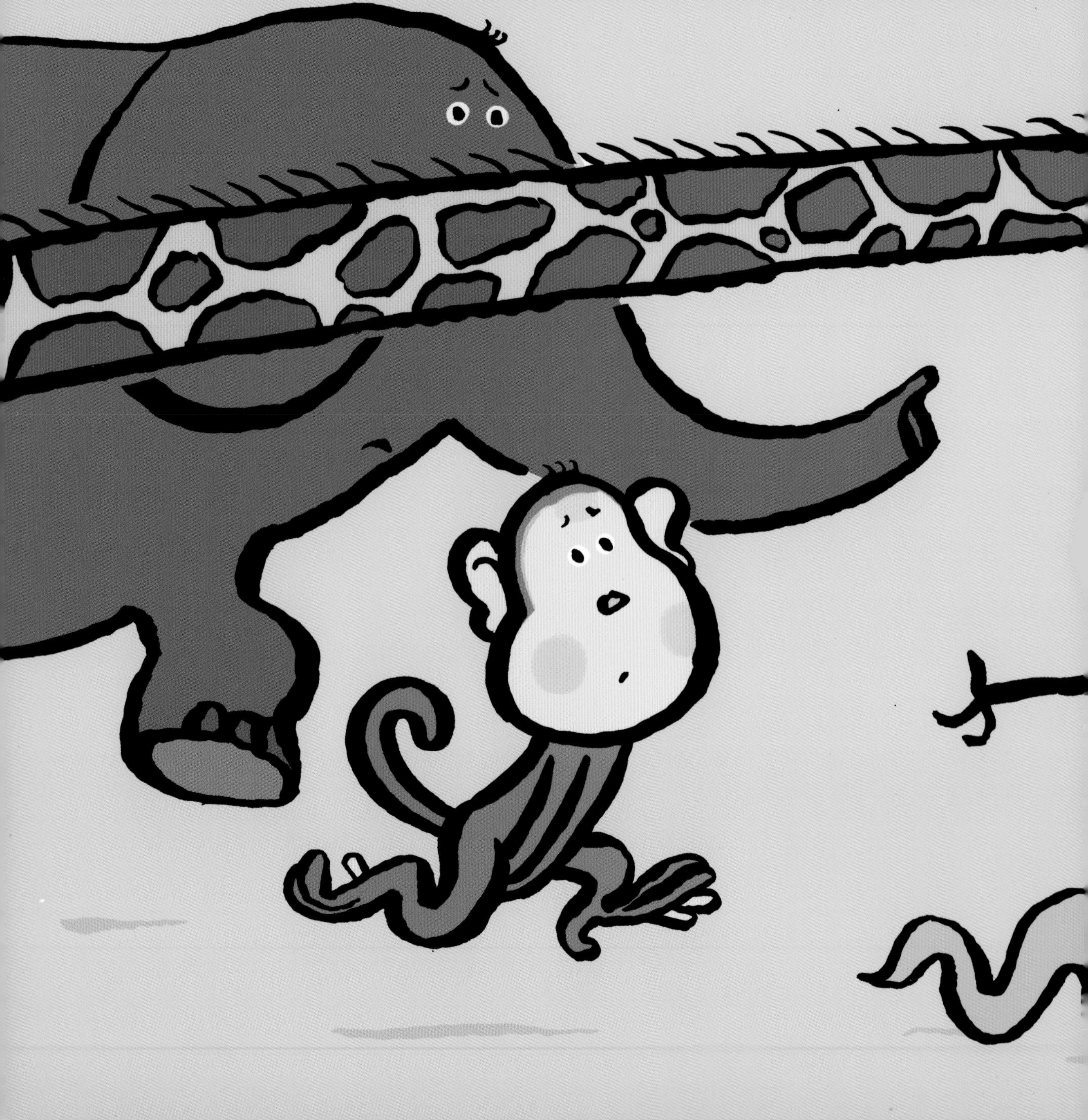

We have to go, too!

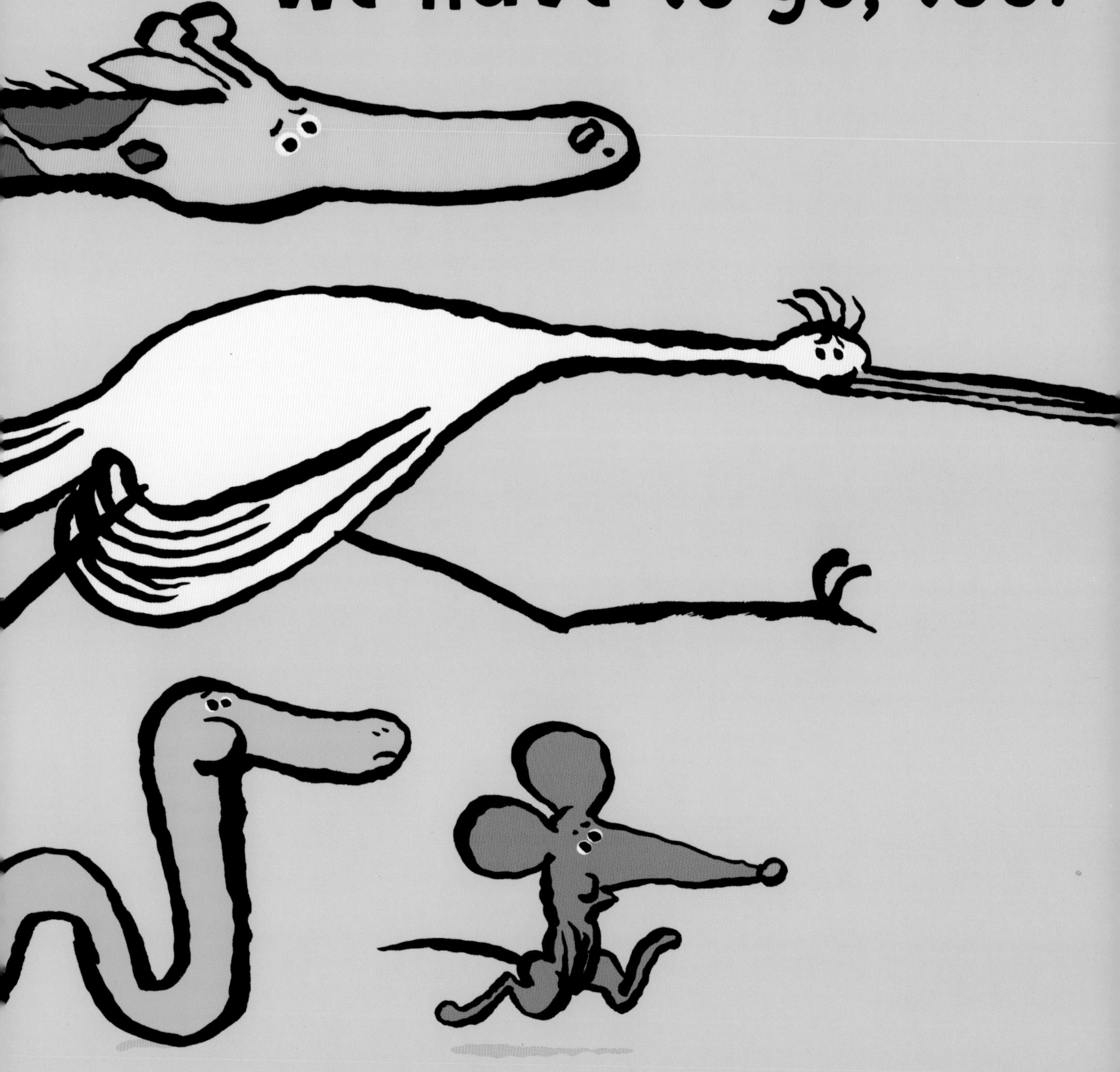

The little bee is buzzing to go as well!

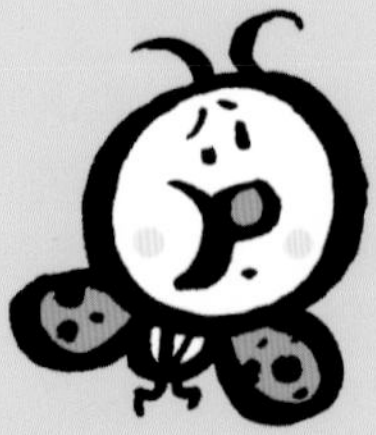

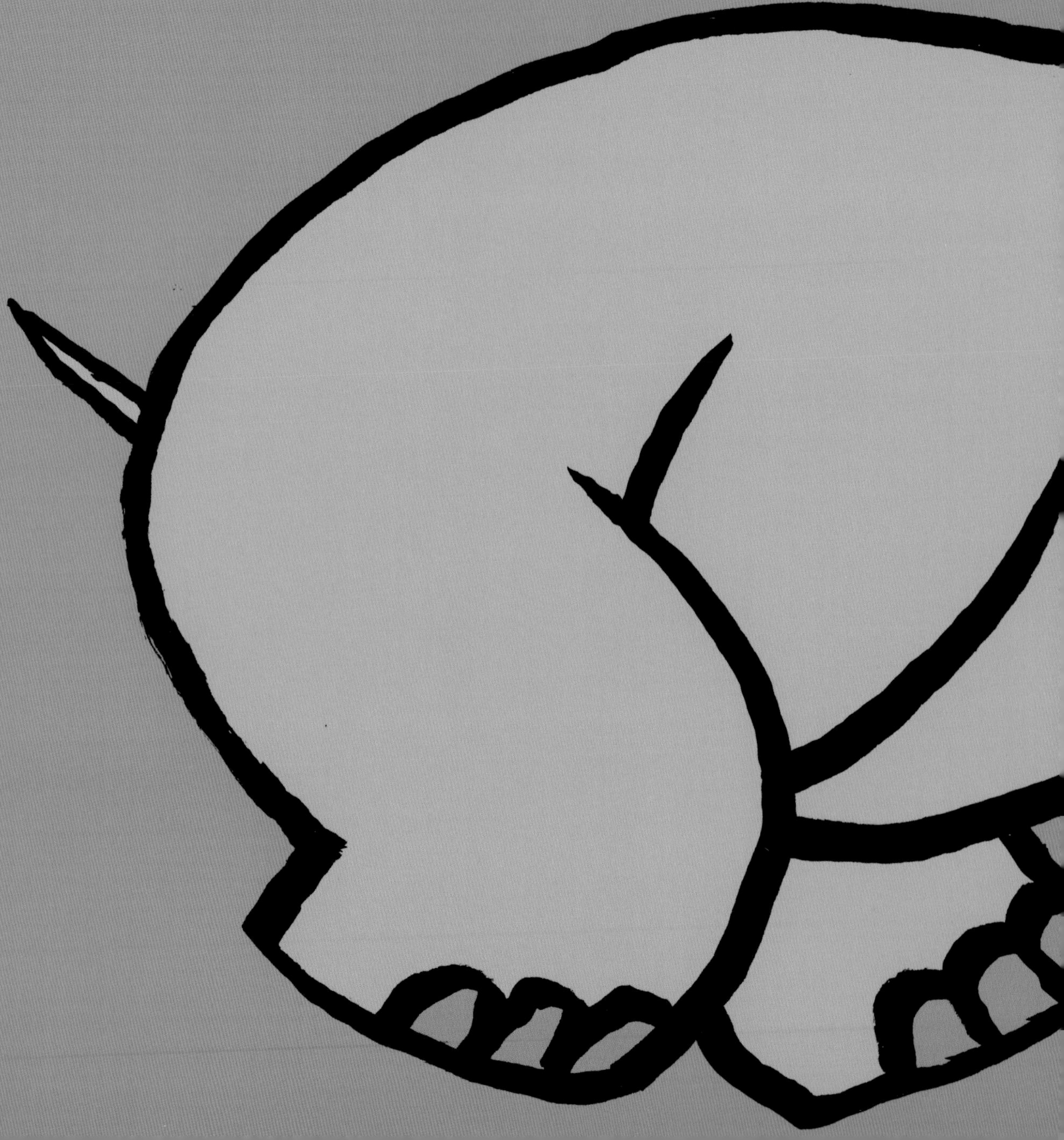

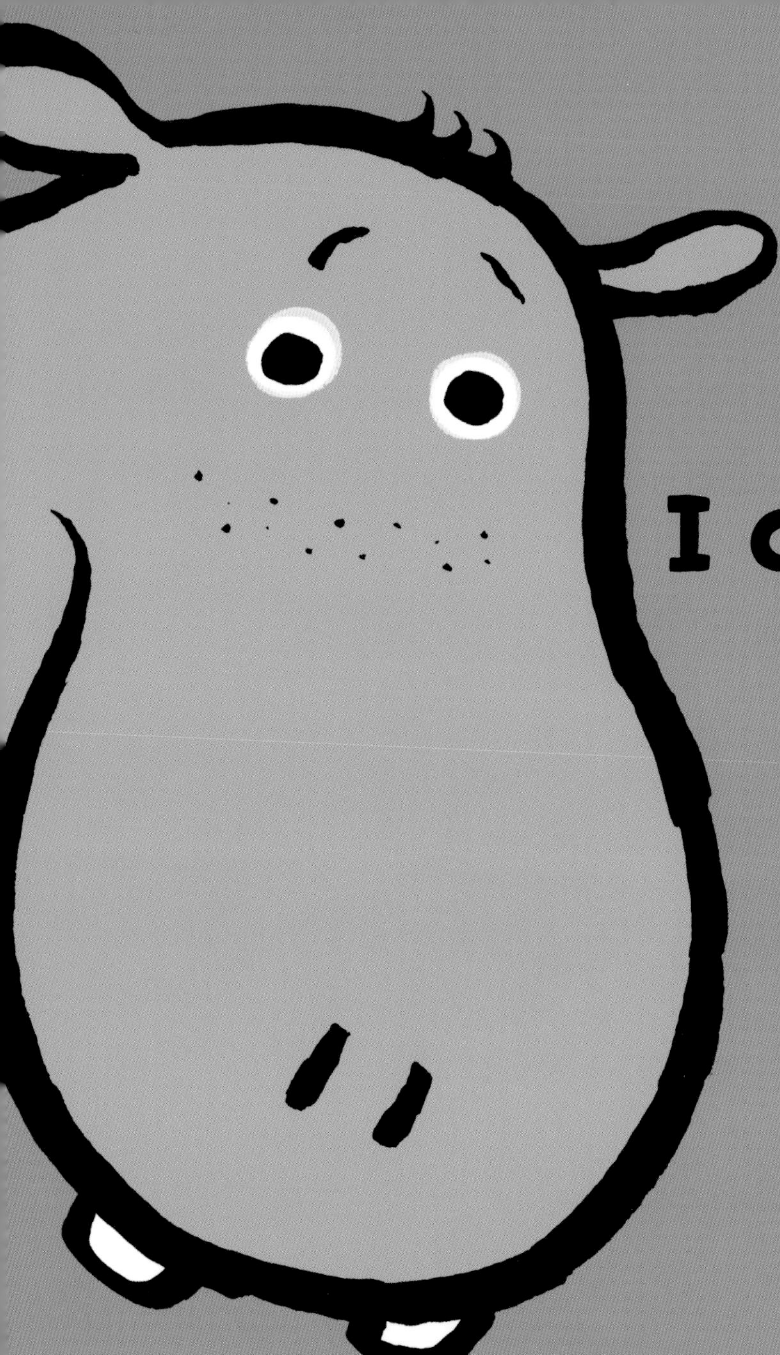

I can’t wait!

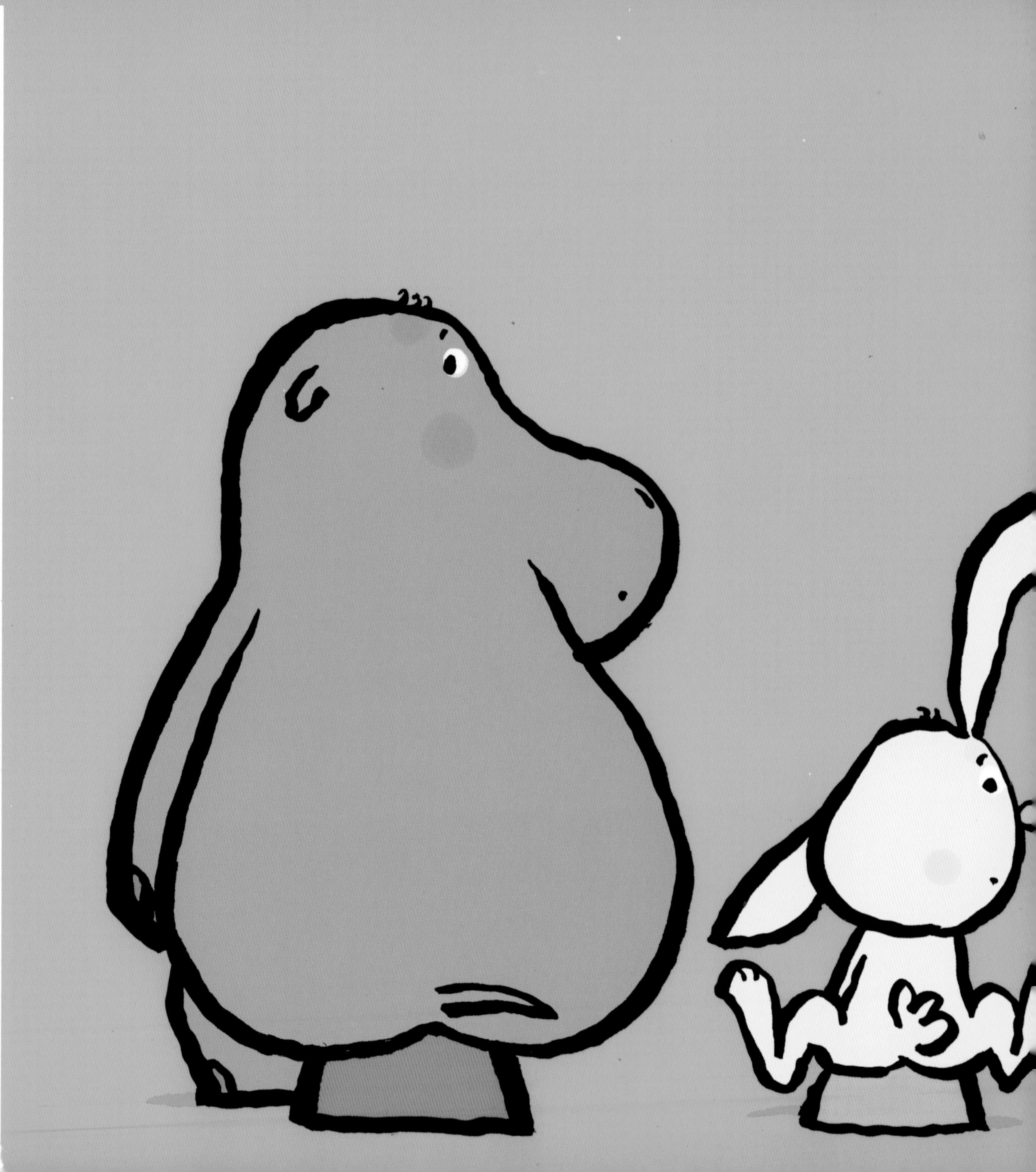

AHHH!

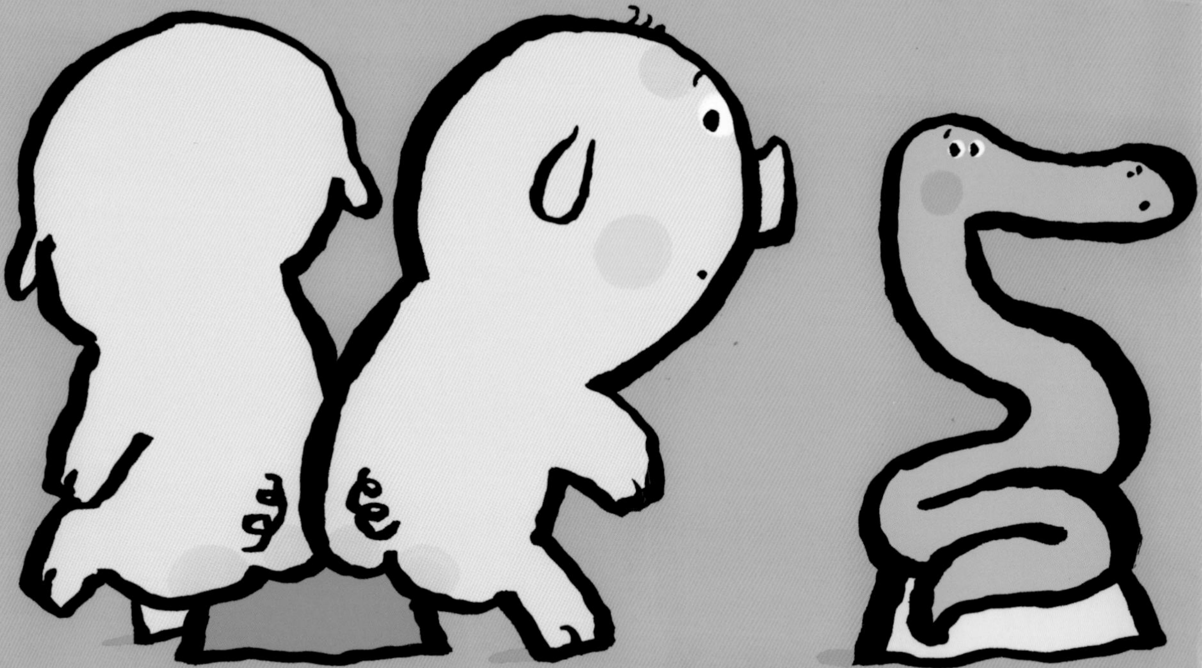

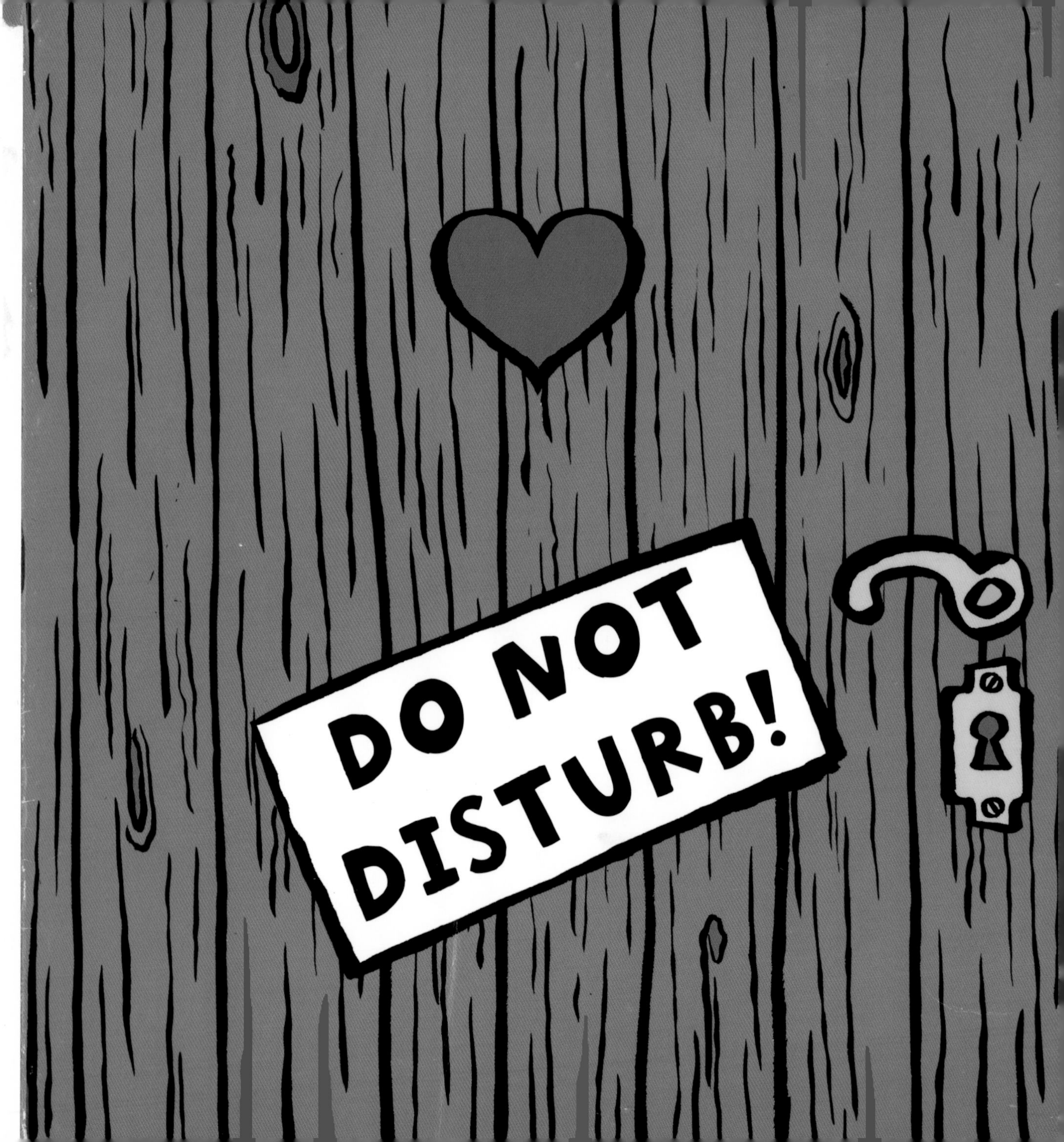
DO NOT
DISTURB!